LIBRARY OF CONGRESS CATALOGING-IN-PUBLICATION DATA:

NAMES: REX, ADAM, AUTHOR, ILLUSTRATOR.
TITLE: NOTHING RHYMES WITH ORANGE / ADAM REX.
DESCRIPTION: SAN FRANCISCO, CALIFORNIA :
CHRONICLE BOOKS LLC, [2017] |
SUMMARY: ALL THE FRUITS GATHER TOGETHER
AND ENJOY A RHYMING PARTY, BUT POOR ORANGE
FEELS LEFT OUT BECAUSE HE DOES NOT RHYME WITH
ANYTHING-UNTIL APPLE INVENTS A NEW WORD.
IDENTIFIERS: LCCN 2016045594 |
ISBN 9781452154435 (ALK. PAPER)
SUBJECTS: LCSH: ORANGES-JUVENILE FICTION. |
FRUIT-JUVENILE FICTION. |
LONELINESS-JUVENILE FICTION. | CYAC:
FRIENDSHIP-JUVENILE FICTION. | FRUIT-FICTION. |
ORANGES-FICTION. | FRUIT-FICTION. |
RHYME-FICTION. | LONELINESS-FICTION. |
FRIENDSHIP-FICTION.
CLASSIFICATION: LCC PZ7.R32865 NO 2017 | DDC
[E]-DC23 LC RECORD AVAILABLE AT
HTTPS://LCCN.LOC.GOV/2016045594

MANUFACTURED IN CHINA.

 MIX
Paper from
responsible sources
FSC™ C104723
www.fsc.org

DESIGN BY ADAM REX AND KRISTINE BROGNO.
THE ILLUSTRATIONS IN THIS BOOK WERE
RENDERED IN FRUIT.

* * * * 10 9 8 7 6 5 4 3   * * * * *

CHRONICLE BOOKS LLC
680 SECOND STREET
SAN FRANCISCO, CALIFORNIA 94107

CHRONICLE BOOKS-WE SEE THINGS DIFFERENTLY.
BECOME PART OF OUR COMMUNITY AT
WWW.CHRONICLEKIDS.COM.

* * * * * * * * * * * * * * * * *
THANK YOU.
* * * * * * * * * * * * * * * * *

Nothing Rhymes With

Rub it in, why don't you.

adam rex

chronicle books · san francisco

Who wouldn't travel anywhere

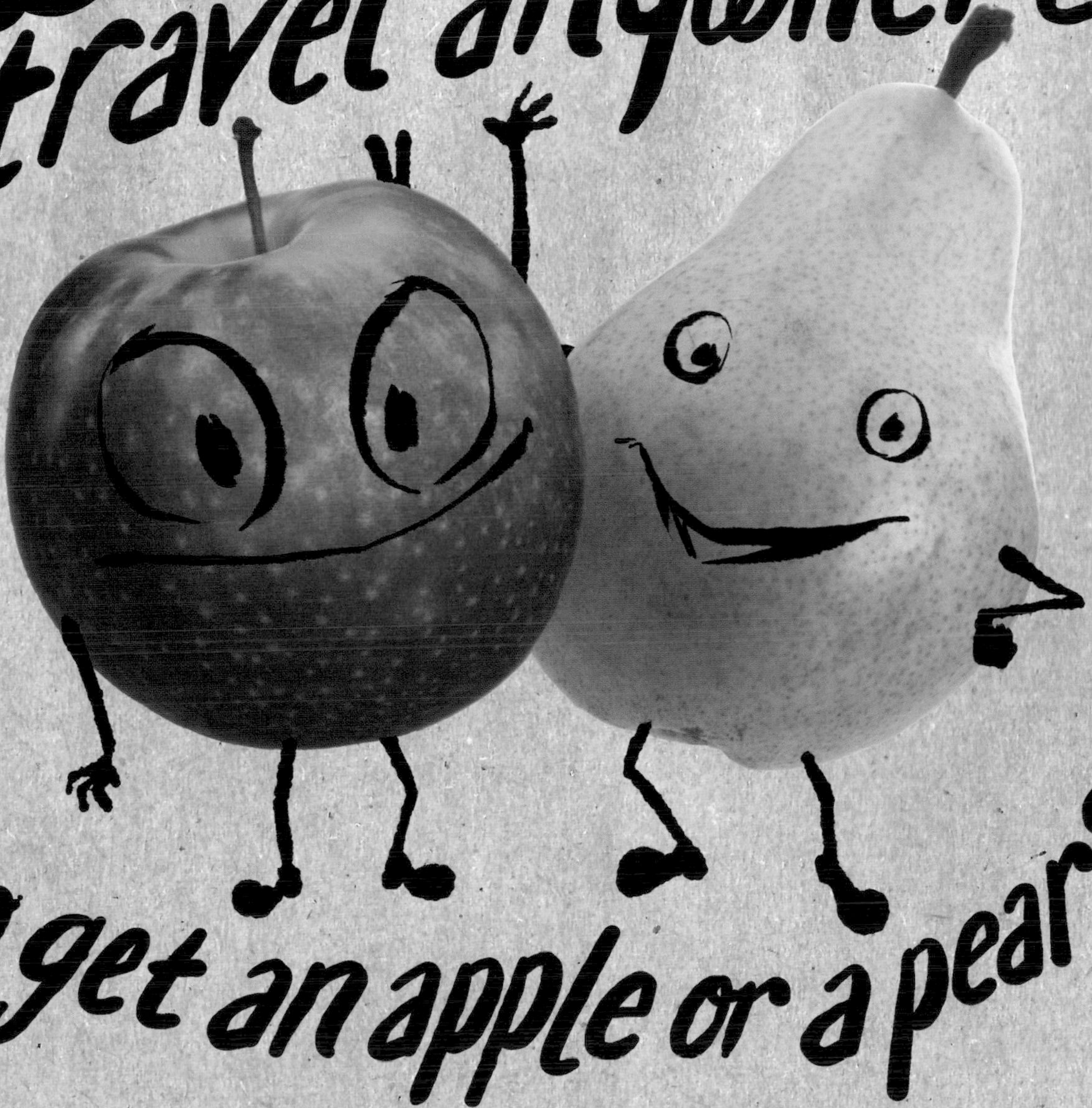

to get an apple or a pear?

And if a chum
hands you
a plum,
be fair and
share that
tasty treat!

It isn't very big, but still I think you'd dig a fig.

I mean, — I know nothing rhymes with me, but—

And this quince wants to convince you that he's really good for lunch.

This what?

I think cherries are "the berries"

and a lychee is just peachy.

Thus Spoke Zarathustra is a book by Friedrich Nietzsche.

What?!

THUS SPOKE ZARATHUSTRA

Friedrich Nietzsche

...is all I'm saying.

If a pear gets lost at night

and meets a wolf, who takes a bite,

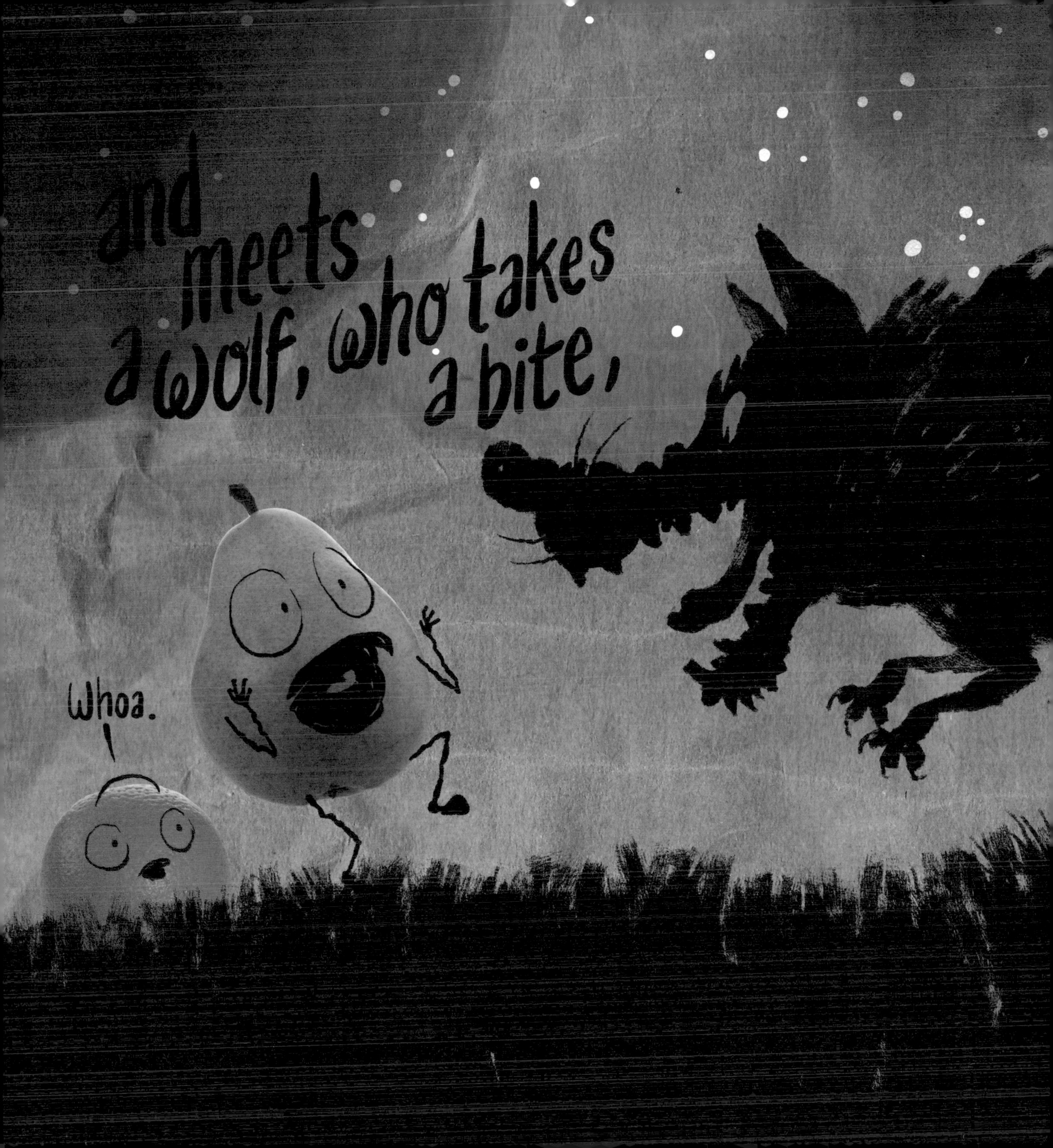

then does that pear become a pearwolf when the moon is full and bright?

This book's sorta gone off the rails.

flies by to tie him to a chair.

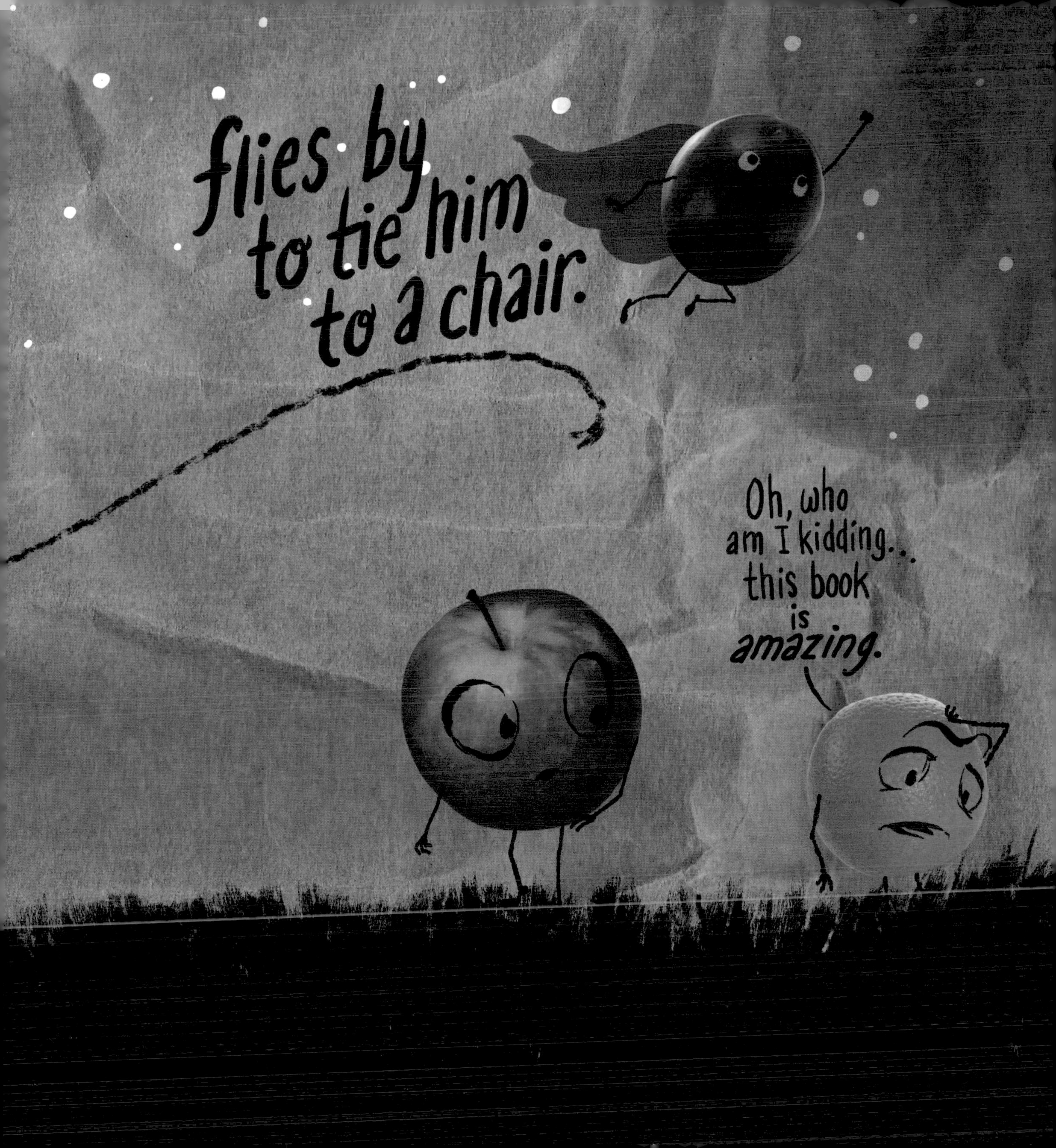

But the fruit are feeling rotten,
'cause there's someone they've forgotten.

It's the orange.
He's really smorange.
There's no one quite
as smorange as
orange.

...Smorange?
What...what
does it mean?

Brute
coot flute
hoot jute loot
newt root toot!

They're healthy happy colorful and cute!

FRUIT
FRUIT FRUIT
FRUIT FRUIT FRUIT
FRUIT FRUIT FRUIT!

SMORANGE!

Fruit feat. Orange
Nothing Rhymes with Orange
Chronicle Records